Story by Sarah Fallon
Illustrations by Alana Shea

Left Behind!

Text: Sarah Fallon
Publishers: Tania Mazzeo and Eliza Webb
Series consultant: Amanda Sutera
Hands on Heads Consulting
Editor: Jess Mackay
Project editor: Annabel Smith
Designer: Jess Kelly
Project designer: Danielle Maccarone
Illustrations: Alana Shea
Production controller: Renee Tome

NovaStar

ISBN 978 0 17 033477 8

Cengage Learning Australia
Level 5, 80 Dorcas Street
Southbank VIC 3006 Australia
Phone: 1300 790 853
Email: aust.nelsonprimary@cengage.com

For learning solutions, visit **cengage.com.au**

Printed in China by 1010 Printing International Ltd
1 2 3 4 5 6 7 29 28 27 26 25

Nelson acknowledges the Traditional Owners and Custodians of the lands of all First Nations Peoples. We pay respect to Elders past and present, and extend that respect to all First Nations Peoples today.

Contents

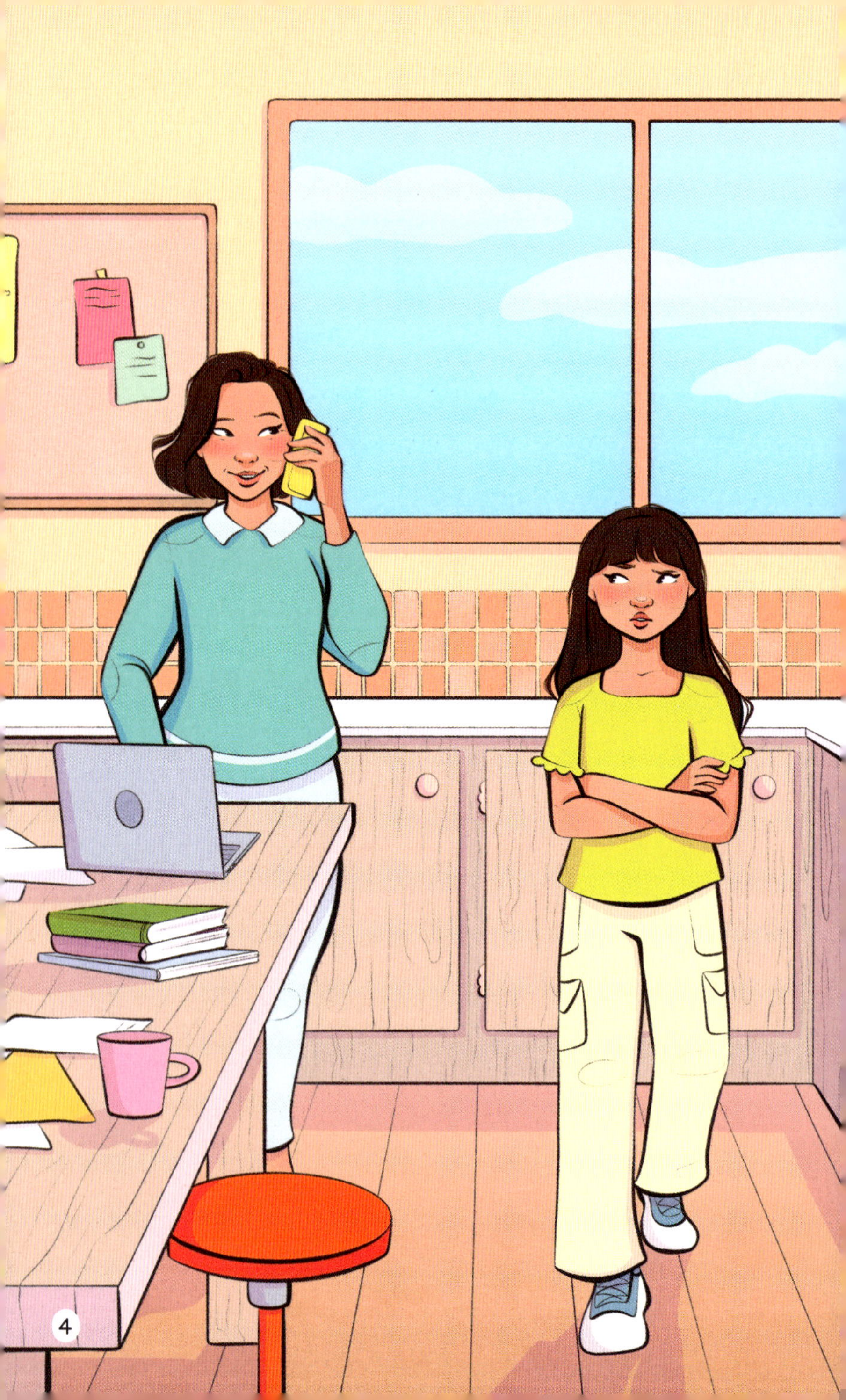

Chapter 1

Getting out the Door

Juniper paced up and down the length of the kitchen. They'd been about to step out the door when her mum's phone rang. Juniper silently begged for her mum not to answer it but, of course, she did. Her mum was attached to her phone these days. If not her phone, it was her laptop, or she was away at meetings.

"Let me just check," Juniper's mum said to the person on the phone. She opened her laptop on the kitchen table. The table had become her office, not just a place to cook and share food together. Papers that were strictly "not to be touched!" were laid out on top of it, and the wall calendar was crowded with work events and meetings.

Juniper had just managed to squeeze the words "Rowan's birthday party" into a tiny corner of today's box on the calendar. No wonder her mum didn't think the party was important.

Juniper groaned. They'd been running late for the party before the phone call. Now they'd be lucky if they made it at all. It was at the new skatepark just outside of town. Juniper had been looking forward to it for weeks.

"Come and sit down," said Trev with a sympathetic smile, as he walked into the kitchen. "You're making me nervous with all that to-ing and fro-ing."

Trev was Juniper's stepdad. He was a bit gruff, but they got on well. He ran a small sheep farm and an engineering business, both from the property where they all now lived. Working from home as he did, Trev was around a lot more than Juniper's mum, but he was usually busy with work. Still, he'd promised to teach Juniper how to ride a dirt bike and that was pretty cool.

Juniper flopped into the seat next to Trev with a sigh. “It’s not fair. She doesn’t care about anyone but herself,” Juniper said.

“That’s not true,” said Trev. “She cares about a lot of people. That’s why she’s so busy with these charities at the moment.”

Juniper rolled her eyes. “Right. She cares about everyone but me.”

Trev did an exaggerated eye roll back at Juniper and she couldn't help but smile. Trev could always force a smile out of her, but it didn't fix things. It was her mum who was supposed to be there for her when she felt down. It was her mum who was supposed to care about things, like getting to parties on time.

Juniper checked the time on her phone: 12.40 pm. They had needed to leave by 12.15 pm to be on time! She sighed again.

Juniper's mum was a teacher-librarian at the local school where Juniper was in Year 6. She was also on a bunch of committees and volunteered for a number of charities. She'd started volunteering after they'd first moved there from the city, as a way to make friends in a new community. But, in Juniper's opinion, it had quickly got out of control.

Even when her mum wasn't at work, her attention was still on all her other commitments. Not to mention all the extra reading she did after hours. At the moment, she was organising a fairy-tale festival at the school, and there were piles of books all over the house: originals and retellings of stories Juniper used to love, like *Little Red Riding Hood*.

Juniper picked up a copy of *Hansel and Gretel* from the kitchen table and flipped through its pages. There was a time, when Juniper was little, that her mum had read this book to her every single night. Juniper had been obsessed with it, drawing pictures of gingerbread cottages and trails of breadcrumbs. She'd even dressed up as Gretel for Book Week.

Now her mum was reading it to other children. It was as if she just woke up one day and decided Juniper didn't matter any more.

Chapter 2

Party Time!

Finally, Juniper's mum ended the call. "Right," she said. "Are you ready to go?"

"Are you serious? I was ready ages ago – when we still would have been on time," Juniper said.

Trev stifled a chuckle.

Her mum looked at the time on her phone: 12.45 pm. "Sorry, hun. Cathy really needed me to send her the presentation right away. There's still plenty of the party to enjoy. Let's get a wriggle on."

Juniper and Trev got up from the kitchen table at the same time.

"I'd better get a move on, too," Trev said. "There's been reports of wild dogs in the area and I need to check the lambs."

Juniper wasn't listening. She grabbed her skateboard and Rowan's present. "Bye!" she called over her shoulder to Trev as she raced to the car.

When they got to the skatepark, Juniper jumped out of the car and ran to join her friends. Her mum gave a short honk from the car as a goodbye before pulling back onto the main road.

"Where have you been?" Rowan laughed as Juniper clipped on her helmet.

"Sorry," Juniper said, "Mum had a phone call."

"Again!" said Indie.

"Again." Juniper sighed.

"Ah well," said Rowan. "Forget all that. You're going to love these ramps. Let's ride!"

The party was just as awesome as Juniper had expected. The new park was massive compared to the old one next to the school. It was clear her friends had been there before and had been practising their moves. But living out on the farm, and with her mum always working, Juniper hadn't been able to get there until now.

Juniper and her friends only stopped skating for some afternoon tea at 2.30 pm. They stuffed their faces with chips and chocolate, and talked about the skate tricks they'd been working on.

When they headed back out, Juniper decided to tackle the vert ramp. She felt like she'd just started when she heard a honk from the car park. She looked up and saw her mum get out of the car and give her a wave. *What is she doing back so early*? Juniper thought. She checked the time on her phone. It was only 3.30 pm. The party didn't finish until 4 pm.

Indie patted her on the back. “Sorry, Junie. Next time we come here, I’ll get Dad to pick you up. Then you can stay as long as the rest of us! I promise.”

“Thanks,” Juniper said, and rode down the ramp. She went around the party saying goodbye to everyone. When she got to the car, her mum was leaning on the bonnet, deep in conversation with Rowan’s dad about the fairy-tale festival. Juniper rolled her eyes and slid into the back seat.

Her mum kept talking. *This is so typical*, Juniper thought. Her mum only cared about herself and her own schedule. If she didn’t need to leave yet, why didn’t she tell Juniper she could keep skating? It was ridiculous. Juniper was sick of it.

Juniper slid back out of the car, leaving her phone and skateboard on the back seat. She strode past her mum without a word and went back out to the ramps. Since she didn't have her skateboard and had already said goodbye to everyone, Juniper drifted to the far end of the park, where a group of older kids were riding. She sat down to watch them.

After a while, the older kids kicked up their boards and left the park. It was probably time Juniper went back to the car, too. She must have been watching the older kids for at least half an hour because the party was clearly over, and all her friends had gone home. How had her mum let her hang out that long?

She headed back towards the car park, but something was wrong. Where was the car? Where was her mum for that matter?

Everyone was gone.

Chapter 3

A Tin Shack

Juniper scanned the park. The whole place was empty except for some guy practising tricks with his cocker spaniel. Her mum had actually left her behind. Juniper couldn't believe it.

Maybe she'd done it on purpose. Maybe she didn't love her any more. It made sense. All the long work hours, all the extra projects. Maybe they were just ways to avoid Juniper. Maybe this had been her mum's chance to get rid of her.

Juniper really wished she hadn't left her phone in the car. What was she supposed to do now? Where could she go?

After a moment's hesitation, she walked in the opposite direction to the man with his dog.

TREATS

Ahead of her was the bush that bordered the park. She and her friends had often played in its fringes, pretending to be explorers or archaeologists. Juniper thought she could probably build a shelter in there. Then she'd have somewhere to sleep for the night. It wouldn't be long before it was dark. She could work out what to do next in the morning. And it was bound to be safer than out in the open of the park, where all the strangers could spot her.

Juniper was still in shock that her mum had actually abandoned her there. Maybe she and Trev had planned it. Maybe that's why they'd been out of the house so much lately. They'd been together, plotting this. Her mum must not love her any more.

Juniper wove through the paperbarks. She went deeper into the bush than she ever had before. In the dirt beneath her were all kinds of forgotten items. She kicked free a bucket hat and an old boot, both stained brown from years of laying half-buried in the dirt.

She went deeper still, finding rusted hubcaps and steering wheels, then finally the remains of an ancient little car nestled in amongst the trees.

She wondered if she could use the old car as a base for her shelter, then decided it was a tetanus infection waiting to happen and moved on.

She started to collect sticks as she went: big ones, as tall as her, that she might be able to build her shelter from.

The wind picked up, whistling through the trees. Juniper shivered. Then the sun hit something shiny beyond the gum trees. It was a tin shack, half rusted in places but solid. This was perfect. She dropped her bundle of sticks. She wasn't going to have to build a shelter after all.

Chapter 4

Dinner Time!

Juniper still remembered when they'd first moved into Trev's house on the farm. It was a few years ago now. Mum had loved it, calling it "cute" and "rustic". Juniper had needed more convincing, but eventually she'd settled in and grown to like it, too. She and her mum took over the small orange-tiled kitchen like a whirlwind, cooking together almost every day, just like they had in the city.

Apart from reading, cooking was their favourite thing to do together. They baked brownies, mixed up muesli and barbecued brisket. But their specialty was a big roast chicken. Or it had been. Now the kitchen was too cluttered with charts and reports and library books for there to be any space to cook.

Now there was no baking.

Dinner was mostly takeaway, or Trev and Juniper would barbecue something. Mum was even too busy to eat a proper meal with them. Her laptop was always open at the table, and she ate with one hand while she typed or scrolled with the other.

Juniper wondered how cute and rustic her mum would find the bush shack. She peered through the open windows, but it was too dim to see.

She pushed open the creaky front door. Once inside, it took a few blinks for her eyes to adjust to the dust-filled gloom.

The room was small and empty, except for a lot of cobwebs and a pot in the corner. Maybe it had been used as a toilet in the olden days. Juniper walked slowly across the creaky floorboards to a door in the far wall. It opened back out into the bush, so she closed it again.

There was one more door to her left. It opened to a second room. In the centre of the room was a wooden dining table and two chairs.

The strangest thing was sitting on the dining table – a roast chicken! Its skin was perfectly golden and glistening.

Juniper looked around for signs that somebody had been there recently. Maybe teenagers liked to come there to hang out and have dinner. Maybe they'd just gone back to their car to get the rest of their food. She could ask them for a lift to a friend's house when they came back.

Juniper couldn't take her eyes off the chicken. Her stomach growled and her mouth started to water. She'd only had chocolate and chips to eat all afternoon, and it was getting late. She stared at the chicken. She knew she shouldn't eat strange food. It could be poisoned or it might've gone bad. But it looked so fresh and delicious.

Chapter 5

Wild Dogs

Juniper tried waiting for someone to come back, but her hunger got the best of her. She reached out to tear a drumstick from the chicken. But then she stopped, her hand outstretched. What was that noise? She stood as still as a statue.

There were sounds coming from outside the shack. Maybe it was the owners of the chicken coming back to eat it? She strained to hear. Her heart started to race. That wasn't the sound of people. It was a growl. A much more animal-like growl than her stomach had made a moment ago. What was it Trev had said on his way out that morning? Reports of wild dogs in the area. Juniper's stomach dropped. Why hadn't she been more careful?

Now it sounded like there was more than one dog growling at a time. How close were they? Could they tell she was inside? How could her mum have left her there to be eaten alive by wild dogs! If Juniper survived, she was never going to talk to her again.

There was a bang that sounded like something jumping on the walls of the shack and the whole thing shook. Juniper looked at the chicken again. She could use it to distract the dogs and get past them. She ripped free the drumstick she'd been hoping to eat. But just as she was mustering the courage to run from the shack, the drumstick raised like a club, she felt something tickle her hand.

She looked up. Crawling down her thumb, towards her wrist, was a big juicy maggot. Juniper threw the drumstick back towards the table in horror. There, spilling out of the hole where she'd torn the drumstick free, were mountains of maggots.

Juniper screamed and ran. The thought that she had almost eaten that rotting chook made her want to throw up. She fled the shack as fast as she could. When she threw open the front door, she looked back and forth through the trees and saw no sign of the dogs.

She ran as fast as she could, only glancing back once. Two scrawny-looking mongrels slunk into the shack, following their noses to the decaying chook. Juniper kept running.

Chapter 6

Lost

Juniper ran until she felt like neither maggots nor wild dogs were chasing her. When she finally stopped, she looked around. The bush was much darker now and the air a lot cooler.

Juniper sat down under a tree. In the dim light, nothing looked familiar. She had no idea where she was, and even if she did, she had nowhere to go. Sitting there, biting back tears, Juniper realised the only person she wanted to find her was her mum.

Juniper remembered that when she was little, before Trev and before this town, it was just her and her mum. It was her mum who would stick bandages on her scraped knees as she learned to skate. It was her mum who held her when she cried. It was her mum who found her when she got lost in the shopping centre.

She remembered the voice-over from the loudspeaker calling her name, telling her that her mum was looking for her; that her mum was waiting for her at the information desk. She remembered feeling certain that her mum wanted her and loved her when they were reunited through the crowds of shoppers.

Juniper's tears fell harder and faster as the loneliness settled in. She wiped them and the snot away with the back of her sleeve. When she opened her eyes again, she saw lights through the trees. They moved along in one direction then turned and came to a stop, shining their full brightness towards the trees. They had to be headlights, which meant they had to be coming from the car park!

Juniper jumped to her feet. She wiped at her eyes again and stumbled through the trees as best she could in the darkness. She burst out into the park at a run. She could see the silhouette of a person against the headlights, and then she heard the distant sound of her mum calling her name.

Chapter 7

Reunited

Juniper's mum started running towards her and they collided in the tightest hug.

Juniper's tears returned and she was surprised to feel her mum start to cry as well.

"Are you okay? Are you okay?" her mum stammered.

"I'm okay," Juniper said between sobs. "I thought you'd left me. I thought you didn't want me."

Juniper's mum's arms tightened around her. "I'm so sorry. I got another call about the fairy-tale festival, and I hadn't realised you got back out of the car. I'm so, so sorry." She pulled out of their hug and looked Juniper in the eye. "I would never leave you," she said with certainty. "I love you. I will always love you." Her mum wiped a tear from her face. "You know that, right?"

Juniper nodded and her tears started to slow. "You've just been so busy lately. It's like you never have time for me."

“I …” her mum started to speak, and Juniper braced herself for another excuse, another reason why her work was more important than Juniper could ever be. But her mum closed her mouth and shook her head. “You’re right. I’ve been distracted a lot lately. I’m sorry you’ve been feeling this way. I’m going to try to do better. Maybe I can cut back on some things.”

“Really?” asked Juniper.

“Yes.” They started walking back to the car. “We can get back to doing some of the things we used to do together, too.”

“I’d like that,” Juniper said, as they got in the car.

“Why don’t we stop at the shops on the way home. We can make dinner together tonight. How about our specialty – a big roast chicken?”

Juniper felt sick at the thought of the chicken back in the shack. "Anything but roast chicken," she said.

Her mum laughed in surprise. "Okay, whatever you want. We can make anything."

"Thanks, Mum. I've missed you."

Her mum smiled. "I've missed you, too."